**To my mother and Itsasne and
every woman who refuses to yield.**

This book's illustration was supported
by the Ramon Llull Institute.

LLLL institut
ramon llull
Língua e cultura catalã

She Rides Like the Wind—
The Story of Alfonsina Strada
by Joan Negrescolor

Translation from Portuguese to English
by Jethro Soutar

Published by Little Gestalten, Berlin 2020
ISBN 978-3-89955-853-1

The German edition is available under
ISBN 978-3-89955-852-4.

Typeface: Futura by Paul Renner

Printed by Print Best, Estonia
Made in Europe

The Portuguese original edition
Eu, Alfonsina was published by Orfeu Negro.

© 2019 Orfeu Negro
© 2019 Joan Negrescolor
© Original text editing: Carla Oliveira
© Original art direction: Rui Silva
© for the English edition: Little Gestalten, an imprint
of Die Gestalten Verlag GmbH & Co. KG, Berlin 2020.

For more information, and to order books,
please visit www.little.gestalten.com

Bibliographic information published by the
Deutsche Nationalbibliothek. The Deutsche
Nationalbibliothek lists this publication in
the Deutsche Nationalbibliografie; detailed
bibliographic data is available online at
www.dnb.de

This book was printed on paper certified
according to the standards of the FSC®

FSC
www.fsc.org

MIX
Paper from
responsible sources
FSC® C129413

JOAN NEGRESCOLOR

SHE RIDES LIKE THE WIND

The Story of Alfonsina Strada

When I was ten, my dad gave me a bike.

This was our first encounter.

The bike was much bigger than me.

Much faster than me.

It went one way, I went the other.

All I wanted was to be free. I wanted to race and ride.

So I stole my grandfather's boots (just for a bit).

And my uncle's trousers (they were there for the taking).

Then all I needed was an imperial mustache.

And the postman's hat.

Outfit complete, I sped off.

I crossed the town square.
Swerved past the general.
Zigzagged left and right.

Then I made my announcement.
I, Alfonsina, will be a cyclist!

I rode up and down the mountain.
I fell off and got back on, over and over again ...

... and I haven't stopped pedaling since.

I won my first race when I was thirteen.

I rode in St Petersburg.

I raced in Bologna, Paris and Lombardy.
I raced here, there and everywhere.

They called me the Pedal Queen.

Faster than the wind,

like an arrow to the finish line.